S0-DUS-320

What Is Dreaming?

VLB Veronica Lane Books

What Is Dreaming?

By Etan Boritzer   Illustrated by Jeff Vernon

www.veronicalanebooks.com email: books@veronicalanebooks.com
2554 Lincoln Blvd. Ste 142, Los Angeles, CA 90291 USA
Tel/Fax: +1 (800) 651-1001 / Intl: +1 (310) 745-0162

Library of Congress Cataloging-In-Publication Data
Boritzer, Etan, 1950-
What Is Dreaming / by Etan Boritzer
Illustrated by Jeff Vernon -- 1st Edition
p. cm.

SUMMARY: Presents children with an understanding of the concepts related to dreams and dream interpretation.

Audience: Grades K - 6

ISBN 978-9762743-7-7 (Hardbound)
ISBN 978-9762743-6-0 (Paperback)

The Library of Congress No.2007934244

...to the children of the world...

What is Dreaming?

Do you remember the story
of the caterpillar dreaming?

The caterpillar was sleeping
on a big green banana leaf,
and she was dreaming about the day
when she would become
a big beautiful butterfly.

When the caterpillar woke up,
she was confused.
Was she a caterpillar
dreaming that she was a butterfly,
or was she a butterfly
dreaming that she was a caterpillar?

Dreams can be confusing
because sometimes dreams seem real!

What is Dreaming?

What is Dreaming?

Do caterpillars really dream?
Do birds dream?
What about your cat?
Does he dream
about chasing a mouse?

Does a giraffe dream?
Does a snake dream?
Does a kangaroo dream?

Does your Mom or Dad dream?
Do you ever talk about your dreams
with your friends?

Do different people have different dreams?
Does a kid in China
have different dreams than a kid in Africa?

Or, is there a dream world somewhere
where we all meet and dream together?

Most everybody,
and probably animals too, dream.
Most everybody dreams at night,
but sometimes we daydream too.
(Are you daydreaming right now?)

Some nights we sleep really deep
and we don't think we have any dreams.
But maybe we *do* have dreams
and we just forget them.

Sometimes we wake up after a dream,
have a glass of water,
and go right back to sleep.
The next morning,
maybe we don't remember that dream.

But what happens to our dreams?
Whether we remember them or not,
where do they go?
And from where do they come?

Where do dreams come from?

Well, sometimes stuff happens to us
like when we're at school,
or when we're playing with our friends
or when we're running down the street
or when we're just hanging out at home.

Hey, a lot of stuff happens
in our lives every day, right?
Stuff is happening to us all the time—
stuff that we see or hear,
stuff that we smell or taste,
stuff that we touch.

And what about all the stuff
that we think about,
and all our different feelings?

And what about all the stuff
that we don't even *know* is happening to us—
like somebody whispering in the next room
which we can kind of hear,
or like sunshine on our faces,
or like pollution, or like a little green *booger*
growing in our nose…

2+2=4

Wow! Where does all this stuff
that happens to us every day—
the stuff that we know about
and the stuff that we don't know about—
where does all this stuff go?

Well, sometimes different pieces
of all the stuff
that happens to us during the day
gets stuck in our brains,
without us even noticing it
or remembering it.

Then, during the night
while we're sleeping,
all the stuff that happened to us
during the day
just starts playing itself back in our brains,
kind of like a video.

But when our brains play back
all the stuff that happened to us during the day,
sometimes it comes out real different
in our dreams.

Maybe when we're dreaming
stuff happens kind of like it happened
during the day.
But sometimes when we're dreaming
stuff happens that can *never* happen
during the day!

Sometimes we dream about the fun stuff
we do during the day
like eating ice cream with our friends,
or playing video games,
or buying some cool new clothes,
or going on a scary ride
at an amusement park.

But sometimes we dream about fun stuff
we don't *ever* do during the day.
We may never climb up a building
during the day like a *superhero*,
but we may *dream* about being a superhero
and climbing up a building,
because maybe we'd really like to do that!

Fun dreams are usually about
things we like to do
or things we *want* to do.

Sometimes when we're dreaming
about all kinds of fun stuff,
maybe *weird* stuff starts to happen
in our dream.
Then, we get kind of confused,
and we want to try and figure out
what that dream really means.

Like maybe one night
you're having a fun dream
where you are flying over your house
or even over the whole city,
and you can see everything
and everybody below you.

But maybe then
as you're flying around having fun,
you start to come down.
Do you land someplace safe?
Or do you land in a deep lake,
or in a tree?

Sometimes a fun dream
can become a scary dream.

Sometimes a dream has a meaning
but it's like a mystery or a puzzle,
and we have to try really hard to figure out
what that dream really means.

Like maybe one night
you have a flying dream,
and at first it's fun,
but then it gets scary.

Maybe you have a flying dream
because you're having some problems
at home or in school,
and you wish that you could get away
from all those problems,
kind of like you could fly over them!

Maybe another night
you have a scary dream
where you're being chased by a big bear.

Maybe there is a bully in school
who is bothering you
and you're afraid of that bully,
so he becomes even scarier in your dream
by becoming a big bear who is chasing you!

Scary dreams are also called *nightmares.*

Do you know why?

Well, I heard that a long time ago
someone had a scary dream,
and he dreamed that a *mare*…

(You know that a female horse
is called a mare, right?)

…anyway, he dreamed that a mare
was standing on his bed
and staring down at him
while he was sleeping!

Well, he got real scared,
and then he woke up
and he decided to call that dream
a nightmare.

And that's kind of how people got to use
the word nightmare for a scary dream.

Scary dreams are usually about things that we *don't* like, or about things that we don't want to have happen to us.

Sometimes we have a scary dream,
and we think it's real
and we wake up sweating, or even crying.
But what can you do about a scary dream,
or a nightmare?

Maybe when you wake up
you can talk to somebody about it,
like to your Mom or your Dad.
And maybe your Mom or Dad will say,
Hey honey, it's OK. It was only a dream!
And maybe that will make you feel better.

Or, maybe you can tell your brother or sister,
or even a friend in school,
about your scary dream.
Then, maybe they'll tell you
about their scary dream.

See, everybody dreams,
fun dreams and scary dreams—
and sometimes it helps you feel better
just to talk to somebody about your dreams.

(Or, maybe you just want to keep
your dream all to yourself.)

Sometimes we can also talk
to a special grown-up person
who knows a lot about dreaming,
called a *psychologist* or a *therapist*,
or a *counselor* —
kind of grown-up words, huh?

That special person
talks to lots of kids and grown-ups
who are not happy about something
and she or he tries to help them.

That person may ask you
about your dreams,
and all kinds of questions
about your everyday life
at school and at home.

Then she or he will try to help you
figure out what your dreams mean,
and how dreams can really help you
to understand any problems you are having
in your everyday life.

Maybe there is something else
you can do to help yourself
if you have a scary dream.

Like, maybe one night you are dreaming
that you're in a yellow submarine
with four funny guys
wearing funny bright clothes
diving deep in the ocean,
and all of you are singing
and dancing in that yellow submarine!

Maybe later in your dream,
if a big purple shark swims up
and tries to eat the submarine,
you can dream
that you and your friends
push a big red button
and the sub pushes away real fast
from that nasty old purple shark!

Yeah, sometimes we can do stuff
to help ourselves in our scary dreams.

Maybe later in your dream,
that big purple shark shows up again
and starts bothering you
and chasing you again.

What if you just look that shark
right in the eyeballs and say:
Hey Shark, this is my dream!
Get outta here!

I bet that shark soon disappears,
especially if you look into his eyeballs
with a little kindness and caring.

See, if you take control of your dream
and do something about the scary part,
you can make that dream
turn out *not* scary—
just like when you are awake,
and *not* dreaming,
you can do something to control somebody
who is scaring you.

It takes some practice to control your dreams
and to make your dreams turn out *not* scary.
But you can do it!
Just like in your everyday life,
if you think about it,
you can do something to help yourself.

So, if you want to control your dreams,
when you go to sleep tonight
close your eyes,
take a few slow, deep breaths…
in and out, in and out…
and then say to yourself,
I'm going to control my dreams tonight!

If you remind yourself every night
before you go to sleep,
I'm going to control my dreams tonight,
pretty soon you'll be able
to see yourself in your own dream,
and you'll remember to take control
of your own dream.

So, if you are flying in your dream,
you can remember to land safely.
And, if you're being chased
by something or somebody in your dream,
you can remember to stop that too.

Maybe now in your dreams
you can also remember
to start helping *other* people
who may need help.

Maybe now in your dreams
everybody is nice to each other—
and not hurting anybody else.

Maybe now in your dreams
there are lots of flowers
and nice clean beaches all around,
and lots of warm sunshine,
and fun stuff to do,
and no one is hungry,
and everybody is really, really happy.

Maybe those kinds of dreams
can come true —
like how the caterpillar got mixed up
about her dream,
but how she kind of knew from her dream
that inside she was really a beautiful butterfly.

Maybe our nice dreams
can even become real
in our everyday lives!

What is Dreaming?

Some people think that dreaming
is just a bunch of jumbled up thoughts
and feelings from all over the place—
that dreams are just like firecrackers
going off at night far away in our brains.

What do *you* think?
Do dreams have meanings?
Can you control your dreams?
There is so much stuff
to know about dreams!

Maybe we just have to keep talking
some more about dreams—
with your Mom or Dad,
or with your friends,
or with some other grown-ups—
since everybody dreams!

So, let's turn the lights off now
and take a few slow, deep breaths.
Let's go to sleep
and see what happens tonight
in our dreams…